# BRICK OF SOUND

BY

## MADISON
## PATE

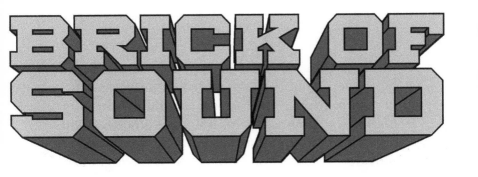

BY
# MADISON PATE

# T&J PUBLISHERS

A SMALL INDEPENDENT PUBLISHER WITH A BIG VOICE

Printed in the United States of America by
T&J Publishers (Atlanta, GA.)
www.TandJPublishers.com

Cover design by Supply Graphics
Book format and layout by Timothy Flemming, Jr. (T&J Publishers)

ISBN: 978-1-7335470-3-1

To contact author, go to:

Website: www.madison-pate.com
Email: contact@madison-pate.com
Facebook: Madison Pate
Instagram: Brick of Sound
LinkedIn: Madison Pate

Special thanks to Ms. Menendez. Thank you for showing me the concept of the brick of sound. This book wouldn't exist without that, or the band entirely.

# TABLE OF CONTENTS

## Chapter 1

## WHAT'S AN EPITOMUS?

I T'S BEEN A MONTH SINCE THE MINI ANNUAL TOURNA-
MENT that we had. It's almost the month of national
band day, which happens to be my birthday! The band
festival is an event that happens every year to show
everyone how strong the future generation of heroes is! Of
course, the greatest hero of them all, who happens to be
my teacher, has been teaching me and my rival, Mandy, for
this past month. Recently, we have been practicing for our
L.G.P.E performance which is 10 days after national band
day. I bet I'll be able to participate in the finals of the festival!

"Hey, get out of my way, extras!" The flute section
leader, Amy said to the brass class that was coming into the
band house.

"You can't just call everyone else extras!" Mandy responded, trying to calm down the situation.

"You're the one who got on top of the tall stand when
Ms. Martinez was choosing low reeds and called everyone
potatoes." Madison said to her, causing Amy to turn towards
her angrily.

"Are you picking a fight with me?" She asked, grabbing Madison by her casual black jacket. In a swift move, Madison grabbed her by her white long-sleeved shirt.

"Sure am!" Madison responded with, causing both of them to get into a mini fight. Chloe walked towards them, and hit both of them on their heads.

"Stop fighting you two! We're about to have an important announcement!" She interrupted, causing them to back away from each other.

"We're sorry." They both said at the same time, causing them to look at each other in complete confusion. Ms. Martinez finally stood up, making the whole room go silent.

"You guys know what time it is? It's Band Festival time!" She said out loud, causing everyone to cheer.

"That means everyone will compete against each other to prove who's the best of the best!" She continued.

"Everyone will show how strong they've gotten in the past month, and I'm proud of all of you!" She finished, then ran back to her office. Chloe looked towards Madison, who was about to start walking off to the flute room.

"So, do you think we'll be chosen as the next low reeds?" She asked her, causing Madison to raise her hand.

"Yeah, as long as you respect your Tenor!" Madison said, giving her a high five.

"And you have to respect your Bari!" Chloe finished for her. Madison then walked off.

Madison reached the flute room, which was always empty. She unwrapped the bandages that was on her right arm from a while ago, which revealed her arm completely healed. There was a small marking on her right palm, which read '3'. She didn't know where it came from but began to think it probably meant something important.

Madison then shook her head. "No way could this mean something." She thought. She began unwrapping the bandages that were on her left arm.

"It's probably just some writing that Mandy drew on me while I was asleep or something." Madison thought again. She looked in the palm of her left hand. Nothing was there. It looked the same as it usually did.

"Oh! I know what it is! It's probably the initials of my b-" She said before interrupted by Mandy loudly kicking down the door.

"Did you hear about the villains from Epitomus targeting us?" She asked Madison, causing her to stand up.

"Uh, no. Don't tell me they're going to do something during the Band Festival." Madison began to worry. Mandy shook her head.

"Yeah, they are. We just don't know when or what they're going to do." She said, sitting down in a chair.

"Wait, I remember something! Weren't you sent to Epitomus before you became a villain?" She asked her.

"Yeah. I remember it like it was yesterday." Madison is suddenly overcome by her memory.

*Flashback*

"This is the last time I'd ever step foot in Epitomus." She thought to herself, sitting down on the ground. But that's what she told herself every time. After getting stuck in that wormhole that was the bridge from Earthland to Epitomus, it seemed like there was nowhere out of this place.

A figure walked up to her and extended a hand. Mandy looked up to them.

"You must be Mandy! I was searching all over for you!" The figure said, revealing that it was actually Chloe.

"You should become a villain with me! We'll shake the world back at Earthland." She said to her, who nodded

and grab her hand.
"It's a deal!"

"I've never been to Epitomus. What's it like?" She asked her. She looked right at Madison.

"Think of like our Earth, but reversed. It's full of trees, and there's villain bases everywhere." Mandy said, getting back up to leave.

"Everyone that we know exists in Epitomus. The only thing that's different about that, is that everyone has their personalities switched." She then said, walking out of the door. Madison looked at her right hand, which still had the 3 in it.

"I wonder how different I am from Epitomus Madison." Madison said, sitting back down.

"I bet she's really cool!"

## Chapter 2

# INTRODUCING MANY PEOPLE

**M**ADISON MADE HER WAY TOWARDS THE MAIN room, which was downstairs. She usually would go out to train that way instead of doing a Mandy and casually jumping out the window with no context. She passed by the Low Reed room, which was always completely wrecked with all of the fights that the current Tenor and Bari have.

"I'm gonna be the best!" Mandy yelled, throwing a chair towards Brayden. He broke the chair in half with just his bare fist.

"No, I'm the best!" Brandon then responded, charging Mandy with the rocket superiority he has.

Madison continued walking. Their fights usually go on for hours upon hours. No one would end up victor, because of how much equal in strength they are. Even though Brandon's power is a Sub-Legendary, named True Strength, he still is equal to Mandy, whose power is also a Sub-Legendary, which is named Blaze.

Madison believes they fight more than she fights with

Mandy, since their fights are basically scheduled now. Everyone knows when to skip by the Low Reed room.

She made it down to the main room, where her mentor was. She basically only teaches her at these times, because Mandy is busy with her fights. She would turn to her.

"Are you ready for your final training until the Band Fest is over?" Ms. Martinez asked.

"Heck yeah I am!" She said proudly, following her out to the front of the band house.

You might be asking right now, 'what's a band house?' It was built for them after they noticed their victory against the strongest villain association, which was way after they defeated them. It has multiple rooms, specifically for sections and other things. Like the Jazz Band room, which they only practice in on Wednesdays, but is used by everyone in that band like every day.

Madison got into her fighting position, which was specifically for users with Power, but her alternate version. 5th generation Power works like this; if their feet aren't connected to the ground on a flat level, any attacks directed upwards would harm the user. I know, it sounds dumb. But great power comes at a great cost when it comes to powers like that.

"Here's your next lesson. You see that 3 on your right hand?" Ms. Martinez asked her, causing Madison to be shocked.

"You know about that?" She asked, showing her the number.

"Of course I do, now listen closely. Your left hand will have a 4 on it right about..." She began. Madison looked at the watch on her right arm, which hit 12:00.

"Now." She then finished. Madison looked at her left hand, which had a 4 on it.

"Uh, does this mean anything?" Madison asked, trying to make sense of the situation.

"It does. Tell me your birthday initials."

"3/4/5. Why?"

"That means you have the most dangerous curse! You probably will forget about it, everyone with a curse does." She explained.

"To activate it, try focusing your energy on the center of your body. Then put your hands together, and charge up your Power energy to 100%. Once you feel the time is ready, you have to say '5!' really boldly."

"That sounds dumb." Madison said, completely dumbfounded.

"Just try it." She finished, backing up some. Madison did what she said, focusing on the center of her body. She got out of her fighting position.

The calm aura of Power, which was blue, came off of Madison. She opened her eyes, and put both of her hands together. The aura increased rapidly, to the point of shaking the ground a little bit. Once the aura stopped increasing, she finally finished this off.

"Five!" She yelled, causing a new-found aura to overwhelm the aura of Power in a spiral form. This continued until she got out of the charging position.

"I told you so! Isn't that a nice form?" Ms. Martinez asked her. Madison looked at her arms, which had some sort of line pattern on it.

"I mean, I guess." Madison said, new to this form. It was very different from what she'd seen before from other powers, but it was a nice addition.

"Every day before the curse's complete activation date, the said user would lose all memory of it." She said to Madison.

"Go ahead, try it out."

"Okay, I guess I'll use this move that a friend taught

me!" Madison said, reeling back her now open hand, with the digit gone. She moved her hand forward, causing a large gust of wind to come out. This left a trail in the ground.

"Hmm...maybe only 25% of it activated." Ms. Martinez thought.

"I'll totally win the festival now!" Madison proudly stated. This is her ticket to the finals, the way she could win.

"Yeah, yeah. Go back inside, it's really late out now." Ms. Martinez told her, causing the curse to go off.

"Okay, see you in the morning I guess." Madison said, walking back inside.

She walked into the door, to see everyone just hanging out. Even Mandy and Brandon were there, when they usually were fighting at this time. In band, basically all of them are a part of a big family. They may have their differences, but they still can get along. Chloe walked up to her and put her arm around Madison.

"The special one is here!" She said to everyone, and the room went into a cheer.

"Uh, am I missing something?" Madison asked her. She turned to her and grinned, the one that would always reassure her.

"It's time for your early birthday party, duh!" She answered, flicking her on the forehead.

"Oh! That's nice!" Madison said, looking around. They must've decorated the room while she was getting that lesson. Mandy walked up to her, and Chloe moved back a little from her.

"Here's my gift." She said, handing her a small box. Madison opened it, and looked inside. It was a Tenor reed. She picked it up.

"Wow, very considerate." She said very sarcastic-like.

"At least I got you something in the first place."

"Shut up."

"Okay." Mandy said, walking off. Madison turned to Chloe.

"What'd you get for me, bro?" She asked, putting the reed in her jacket pocket. She took out a small piece of paper. "I got you this, bro." She said, handing it to her. She took the paper and looked at it. On the paper was a single letter. This letter was 'h'. Madison began laughing, and Chloe joined her on this.

"Thanks bro!" Madison said, giving her a high five.

"No problem, bro!"

She walked over to her seat, where she was awarded a crown like hat. It would have to go onto her ponytail, since it wouldn't stop falling off.

"A birthday party, huh?" She said, sinking into her seat. Someone picked up her seat from under her, causing her to sit back up.

"Hey! You should be enjoying the party!" A familiar voice said to Madison, making her look down. It happened to be Allie, the section leader of the Tubas. She jumped down from the chair that was in the air.

"I'm enjoying the party! Just in my own way." Madison said.

"Well, then your way is horrible."

"Shut up. Did you even bring a gift?"

"Perhaps." She said, handing her a box. Madison opened the box, which literally had nothing in it. She looked back up to her.

"Are you joking?" Madison asked her.

"Your present will be in your dreams." She said, then walking off.

"I could use this box anyway." Madison said, putting it in her pocket. She continued walking around.

"Powerful Takedown!" Another familiar voice said from behind her, causing her to automatically turn around and use a small blast to hit them with. Madison caught them while they were falling.

"Aww, not again!" Her friend Ashlyn said to her, making her lift her up.

"That makes it 100-0!" Madison said proudly.

"You only win because of that dumb power!"

"You only lose because of you copying my attack!"

"Both of you, calm down already." Chloe said to them, causing Madison to look away.

"Yeah, calm down." A familiar voice said from behind her.

"Shut up, metal brain! Was that a threat?" Madison asked her friend Alex, who was the one who said it.

"Yeah it was! Do you have a problem?"

"How about the both of you shut up!" Mandy said from afar, throwing a box at her. She caught the box.

"No, you!" Madison responded with, throwing the box back. This continued until Ms. Martinez walked into the main room.

"All of you need to go to bed!" She said to everyone, causing them to all go back to their sections' rooms.

Madison walked upstairs to the flute room, which was literally still completely deserted, even though there are other flutes than her. She got onto her bed, which had a note on it. Madison picked it up and unfolded it. The note read 'homie handshakes.' She laughed at the note and put it down on her desk.

"Wonder who wrote that." Madison thought.

———————————

Later that night, Mandy walked by the flute room, to see Madison still sleeping. She quietly opened the door. She walked up to the bed that she was on.

"Disable!" She shouted, punching Madison straight in the stomach. This woke Madison up.

"Hey, what the heck are you doing? I was having a good dream!" Madison shouted at Mandy, somewhat angry.

"I was wondering why you were asleep for so long! You usually wake up before me!"

"That's none of your business, you h!" Madison said, making Mandy grab her by the arm and drag her downstairs.

"Shut up, we're going to the store and you're going to like it."

# BRICK OF SOUND

## Chapter 3

## BEFORE THE FESTIVAL

HOW MANY TIMES WILL THINGS LIKE THIS HAPPEN? So, a person shows up- scratch that- basically crashes down in front of the band house, and happens to look like Section Leader? Why the heck would that just happen completely out of the blue?

"Are you.... Madison?" "Section Leader" asked her, causing Madison to look a little confused.

"Uh, yes and no. I am Madison, but I'm not your Madison." Madison answered.

"What do you mean?"

"You see, you're from Epitomus, and somehow you're in Earthland."

"Oh."

"Sorry to break the conversation, but how did you get here?" Mandy asked her. She looked down, seeming to be thinking.

"The last thing I remember was being blasted by the person who terrorized our people." EP Chloe said, beginning to look serious.

"And who was that?" Chloe asked her.

"The 'Destroyer', Allie." They all looked towards Allie in some form of disbelief.

"Hey, she's talking about Epitomus Allie, not me!"

"That's believable." Madison said to her.

"Anyways, what's she done to you guys?" Mandy asked her.

"She took away our only chance of winning and stole my Madison's power." She told her, causing Madison to shudder.

"I can't imagine losing what took me forever to get." Madison said in response, as EP Chloe nodded.

"My Mandy doesn't take that too well either." She said, right after Madison and Mandy looked at each other, then both at her.

"What's our relationship in Epitomus?" They asked at the same time.

"Well, in Epitomus, you guys basically love each other." EP Chloe answered, causing them to both look sick.

"No way, I'd never think that way of that idiot!" Mandy said.

"Yeah, I agree with her!" Madison agreed.

"Ignoring those two," Chloe began, shoving them both out of the way.

"Who or what was your only chance of winning?" She asked her.

"It was Ms. Martinez. She saved us all from doom before but now she's just gone." She answered. Mandy and Madison looked at each other for just about the 50th time that day.

"Just imagine how hard it would be without her." Madison said, with Mandy nodding in agreement.

"Yeah, I can't."

"Wait, where actually is Ms. Martinez?"

"She's probably eating Oreos in a parked car."

"Makes sense."

After a few minutes of talking, they all came to an agreement. The day after the tournament, they would head out to Epitomus to put a stop to EP Allie. Or at least try to. But who knows, will they succeed?

Madison had walked back to the flute room, when stopped by EP Chloe, who was still overwhelmed with the new environment.

"So, what do I call you?" She asked her. Madison was confused by the question, but still would think about it.

"Call me Madison!" Madison began. She then thought about what she said.

"Or Mandy 2.0, whichever suits your likings." She finished.

"So, what's with you and Mandy? Are you guys friends?" EP Chloe asked her.

"Yeah, I guess we are. But we don't get along very well. I sometimes think of her as a big brother!" Madison said for some reason really proudly.

"Well anyways, I have a big event soon, so I need to get some sleep." She said, beginning to walk away.

"Hope to see you tomorrow at the festival!"

"Big brother…." EP Chloe began to say to herself.

"…that's something she would think of."

# BRICK OF SOUND

## Chapter 4

## THE STARTING LINE

EVERYONE GATHERED INSIDE OF THE BAND ROOM, waiting for the all call to head to the arena.

"Looks like everyone's here, but where's Madison and Mandy?" Ms. Martinez asked everyone, looking around. Suddenly a window shattered. It showed Madison and Mandy in their band outfits and Mandy with her signature stop sign.

"You all suck!" Mandy said, landing on the ground.

"I'm the future hero of you all!" She finished.

"Yeah, future oboe."

"Shut up, dummy!"

At the band festival, everything was very lively. Just about everyone was there. Even the brass was there. During the band festival, they got a speech from whoever is seen as the top of the class and they're allowed to say anything. This time Mandy was allowed on the stage.

"This is a bad idea…." Madison thought to herself.

"Alright, listen to this you weebs!" She announced to everyone.

"I'm gonna be the best, and if the luck goes in my favor, that's going to happen!" She finished, causing everyone to be dumbfounded.

"Mandy, you can't just say that!" Chloe said from below.

"At least get me down from this thing."

Fast forwarding to the beginning of the festival, they started off with a race. This time, Ms. Martinez gave them a count off.

"Three...Two.... One.... Go!" She said, causing everyone to begin running. Mandy used flames to charge forwards, with Brandon following close behind. Madison grabbed her arm and used a blast from the other arm to charge forwards, still behind them.

"Out of my way, 'Stupid Tenor'!" He said, blasting Mandy from behind.

"No way, 'Oversized Alto'!" She responded with, using blazes to burn him. Madison used this opportunity to break them apart and blast in between them to go forward.

The first obstacle had appeared. It was a large robot that towered above everything, even the arena. Mandy and Brandon saw this as a competition. Mandy blasted upwards and use flames to attack the robot with her signature move.

"Heat Phalanx!" She said, using the flames as assistance to get her fist to do more damage.

At the same time, Brandon used rockets to blast himself upwards in a spinning formation. This is what activated the full power of the Rocket superiority. Once he was fully in the air, he reeled back a fist which had some sort of wind effect to it.

"Impact!" He said, using the wind force to cause extra damage to the robot. They both still were in the air.

"You call that an attack?! How weak are you?" Brandon asked Mandy, who then blasted forwards.

"Weak enough to be stronger than you!" She responded with.

"Hey, get back here!" He said, following her with blasts. Madison still was on the ground. She then got an idea.

"Shiny Tornado!" She said, using two large blasts at the back of her to go forwards really fast. She began to spin, using ideas from the two low reeds as an attack. This 'new attack' was a success, because she managed to make it in front of Mandy and Brandon.

Chloe appeared behind the two out of nowhere. They both looked back at her in fear. It was obvious that she was being mind controlled by Allie, since she was carrying her.

"Want to work together for a second?" Mandy asked Brandon, looking over to him.

"If it's a few seconds, yeah."

"Alright, I want you to push them back using that dumb Impact of yours, and then I'll use my new move. Got that?"

"Yeah, whatever. Impact!" Brandon said, using an attack by wind force to knock both parties back. Mandy put both of her hands together, causing a spiral like blast to begin forming.

"Shining Star!" She yelled, using the blast to blind the others behind them. Brandon grabbed her arm and continued using blasts to propel themselves towards Madison. She looked behind her.

"Oh frick!" She thought before the disaster happened.

"Go flying!" Brandon said, using a rocket to throw Mandy towards Madison. Once they collided, they both crashed down to the floor.

"Get off me, loser!" Mandy said to her. Madison got off of her and helped her up.

"Shut up!" She responded, blasting away. Mandy began following her, but once she reached the air, she was hit in the back by Brandon running into her.

The second obstacle appeared. This time, it's another robot. An even larger one than last time. Madison grabbed her arm, and aimed her open hand towards the robot.

"The bigger they are, the harder they fall!" She said, firing off a large blast. This blast knocked the robot over backwards. This blast caused Madison's arm to begin bleeding, since the larger the blast is, it harms the user to a certain degree.

She ignored the pain and used blasts from her feet to head towards the finish line. Once she made it, she got on her knee to pull out some bandages she had in her pocket and wrapped it around her arm.

"The winner is Madison from the Woodwind Class!" Ms. Martinez announced on the microphone. This caused a cheer from the crowd. Mandy and Brandon followed sometime after, both looking somewhat banged up due to crashing into each other.

"Let's not tell that to anyone." Brandon said to Mandy, who nodded.

"Yeah."

Once everyone finished, they were given a break. Madison went to her waiting room to practice some of her smaller attacks and perfect them. Once she finished, she began to go outside to check out the clouds, for some reason. But she stopped, since she saw two people talking.

"Who do you think has that power?" Ashlyn asked Mandy, holding up a beat-up book with simply the numbers, 345. Mandy took a look at the book again.

"This power is something a monster would have."

"But it has a stupid name." Mandy finished. Madison would look at her left hand, which had the 4 still on it.

"Is this a book about me?" She thought to herself. Mandy took a look inside of the book. All that was inside it were how the curse is inflicted and how it works.

"Are you sure you got this from Epitomus?" Ashlyn asked her. Mandy looked up at her and closed the book.

"I mean, aside from Madison, you're the only person that I could think of that would have some knowledge about it."

"I'm not dumb like she is."

"I'm sure Madison thinks the same about you." She said, walking off. Madison began walking back to her waiting room.

"I hope you win the tournament, Mandy!" Ashlyn responded. Mandy stopped in her tracks.

"Even though I know I will be the best, you should give that advice to Madison instead." She said, then continued to walk off.

Once Madison made it back, she sat down into her seat and looked at both of her hands. The 3 and 4 were still there.

"It really is a curse, isn't it?" Madison said to herself. She thought of how Mandy somehow got her hands on the book. It's probably ages old, since Epitomus had curses before powers.

"25% Blaze!" Mandy said from outside of Madison's room. Because of how bad she is at going below 100%, she ended up blasting through Madison's door and crashing into Madison, knocking them both to the wall.

"This is the 2nd time today, why does this keep on happening?" Mandy questioned her, somewhat angrily.

"I don't know, maybe it's because you're stupid!" Madison retaliated, getting back up.

"You're dumb!"

"Shut up!"

# BRICK OF SOUND

## Chapter 5

## MY STEEL IS UNBREAKABLE

MADISON GOT OUT OF HER CHAIR. IT WAS TIME FOR the match, which happened to have her fighting first. She made it down to the arena and got to her side.

"On the right we have Mandy 2.0, and our winner for the race, Madison!" Ms. Martinez announced, as she walked on to the arena.

"And on our left, we have the only boy flute, Alex!" She then announced, as he got onto the arena. Madison grabbed her arm again, the bandaged one, and pointed it towards him.

"I'm going to make this quick, because without plants, you're just a hunk of metal!" Madison said to him. Alex put both of his fists together.

"Good luck with that, cause my steel is unbreakable!" He responded.

"Alright you two, you may begin…." Ms. Martinez began to say.

"Now!" She finished. Madison had power go specifically into her index finger.

"Burst!" She shouted, sending a huge wave of power towards Alex. He turned his arm into steel to block this attack.

"Are you joking? That isn't your full power!" He retaliated, then charging towards Madison. She charged towards him also, at the same speed. He began to go into his full steel mode, which she noticed and stopped running. Once he got close, she punched him straight in the gut, which made him cough up blood. This sent him flying back to where he originally was.

In the audience, Mandy watched this.

"Since when could Madison use blunt attacks like that?" Mandy asked herself. Chloe looked at her.

"Power works in several different ways. This just is another sub category." She said to Mandy. She looked at Chloe, somewhat shocked.

"Another sub category? She already used a new one!" She said in response. Madison began generating a small blast in her hand.

"That all you got, metal head?" She taunted.

"Not even close!" He responded, charging towards Madison for the second time.

This time, once he got close, Madison dodged his punch.

"Big H!" She yelled, using the blast to send him back, which didn't work. Madison backed up.

"It's Madison time!" Madison jumped in the air, launching herself towards him with two blasts charged in her hands. Alex turned his right arm into platinum.

"Prepare to lose!" He yelled, and Madison used the blast in her left arm to send herself behind him. With her other hand, she fired off a blast towards him. She charged up more blasts in her hands and constantly blasted him.

Every single blast was stronger and stronger until

she got to the point that it could potentially hurt her, so she stopped. The smoke cleared, and it showed Alex on the ground, battle damaged from the blasts.

"The winner is Madison!" Ms. Martinez announced. As smoke came off of her hands, she laughed a little.

"Loser!" Madison walked off from the stadium, heading back to her waiting room. Mandy noticed this and decided to follow her to where she was going.

Madison sat down in her chair, and picked up a notebook on her table that was labeled 'Power Notes'. She added in something about the new fighting attack she came up with and put it down.

Suddenly, Mandy kicked down the already damaged door. She just looked at her, not really caring.

"Why are you always one step ahead of me?" Mandy finally said, slamming her hands on the table.

"Because I am." She responded with, getting out of her chair.

"Hey, this is serious!"

"If it's serious, then act like it." Madison said to her. Mandy used a blast to charge at Madison. It ended up with her on the wall.

"Okay, I'm listening."

"Every time I train to come up with a new move, you always end up with a completely different attack style!" Mandy said, firing off a blast from her hand, which was right next to Madison.

"Why can't you just give me a chance to catch up to you?" Mandy then asked her. Madison looked at her bandaged hand.

"I mean, the only reason why I'm the better one is because of this power." She finally said.

"If I wasn't chosen to have it, I never would've met you or the others." Madison continued.

"And I also wouldn't be alive. It's saved my life in many situations."

"I also don't know how to use it properly. The person who taught me died before they could teach me anything else aside from how to use it." She continued, counting off things on my fingers.

"I have a curse too. It leaves a big weight on my shoulders for me to carry. The name i-" She was interrupted by Allie walking into the room again.

"Hey, do you know where Mandy went again?" She asked Madison, then seeing the situation and taking it completely out of context again.

"I'll just go." She said, then leaving. Mandy moved her hand away from Madison and began walking out.

"Talk to you later, weeb."

"Shut up or I'll send you back to the school!"

## Chapter 6

# LUCK AGAINST SKILL

**M**ADISON BEGAN WALKING INTO THE SPECIAL section for the band kids and sat in a seat, right next to Mandy. Mandy looked at her.

"We might have to go to Epitomus soon." She said to Madison, who nodded at her statement.

"Yeah. Just try not to blow up anything."

"Are you calling me an idiot?"

"Perhaps."

"It's time for the second fight! On our right we have the only clarinet participating, Kelli!" Ms. Martinez announced. She walked up onto the arena.

"And on our left, we have the first chair flute, Amy!" Ms. Martinez also announced.

"Did you know that anyone who goes against me always loses?" Amy said to Kelli.

"Same here!" She'd respond.

"Begin!" Ms. Martinez finally said. Kelli would use water from her power to launch towards her. Amy would use a blast directed towards the ground to dodge it. She kept on sending small waves of water until Amy was in the air.

"Exploding Toilet!" She shouted, sending a huge spray of water upwards to hit Amy. Once it hit her, it trapped her in a prison of water. To keep this prison of water, she raised both of her hands.

Amy saw this as an opening. She began to charge up a large explosion of energy. Once some of the water began to evaporate because of the heat, she released a large explosion.

"If she doesn't hold back with any of her attacks, who knows what'll happen." Madison said, adding more things to one of her notebooks, labeled 'Orange Juice Recipes'.

"Uh, where do you buy your notebooks?" Mandy asked her. Madison looked at her with her usual blank expression.

"A cooking store, why?"

"Why the heck would you buy notebooks from the cooking store?!"

"Cause I can."

Amy would drop down back on the arena floor. Kelli would put her hands together.

"If that's another attempt at defeating me, then it won't work." She said, waiting for the perfect time to launch another attack. Kelli would surround herself with large amounts of water.

Amy just saw this as another opening. But, she didn't attack her. Instead, she just waited. All of the water shot up to the air, keeping its form.

Kelli used water to appear at the bottom of her feet to shoot towards Amy. She waited until she was close enough.

"Short Ranged Shot!" She shouted, launching an attack from her hand that started from the bottom and hit her right in the center. This blast sent her flying backwards, so she caught herself by using her hand to stop the movement.

This process kept on going. She never stopped

charging, until she lost all of the energy she needed. She put her hands together again.

"Crashing Rain!" She shouted, sending the large water that was still above them crashing down in big water droplets. Amy simply lifted up her right arm.

"Large Radius Shot." She said, sending off an extremely large blast, larger than what Madison could do at her full power. The water was disintegrated by mainly the blast, but the heat aspect is what really did the trick. The wind force that came off of this blast knocked Kelli back.

Instead of using her hand to stop her from moving, she still kept on going until she just lost the momentum and fell down. She then tried to get back up. Amy did her evil smirk that she only used when fighting someone equal to her.

"Oh! Is there still some fight in you? Or are you just gonna keep this up forever?" She asked her, then charging towards Kelli. She tried charging towards her, but she lost her balance and fell down. Amy stopped running.

"I won't lose…" She said, then falling unconscious from extreme loss of energy.

"The winner of this match is Amy!" Ms. Martinez announced, causing a cheer from the crowd. She simply just walked off the arena and off to the special section.

Once she got there, she sat next to Alex.

"How could you use an attack like that on someone you know was weaker than you?" Alex asked her. She kept her unbreakable look forward.

"What part of her was weak?" She asked him.

"Personally, I think she's weak enough to be stronger than you."

"You're going to fight Madison. If you lose, I will laugh." Alex said to her.

"I'll never lose to her. Don't you remember? Every time I fought her, she lost." Amy responded.

"Doesn't mean she hasn't improved."

"That doesn't matter. I'll always win, no matter the circumstance."

"Okay, whatever you say."

Madison went back to her room to add more things to her oddly named notebook. It ranged to things from 'Mandy likes to copy attacks.' to literally just 'h'. Once she was done, she got out of her chair and started practicing her moves.

"So, my first move was something like this." She said, making a gun sign with her hand and shooting off a small blast.

"And then, after that I could use a move like this." She continued, charging power through her right hand and punching the air.

"And after my training, I can now do this!" She finished, sending off a sharp gust of wind with her finger.

"Looks like you've gotten stronger, bro!" Chloe said, walking in the room and fist bumping Madison.

"Heck yeah! I bet I'll eventually become stronger than how Ms. Martinez was in the past!" Madison responded.

"Even though that's almost impossible, I still believe you, bro!"

"Thanks, bro!"

"Wish me luck in the next round, bro!"

"Okay, bro!" Madison said, then giving her a high five. Chloe eventually left the room, after constantly calling each other bro over and over. Once she left, Mandy showed up for basically the 100th time that day.

"Hey, do you think Epitomus still has stop signs?" She asked Madison, casually for some reason.

"Why would I know if they still had stop signs? I've never been there!" She responded.

"Well, I'm gonna need a stronger one. Cause Epitomus Chloe said that 'the Destroyer' is on her way."

"Okay. If she shows up during the tournament, that'll be fine."

"Why's that?"

"Because I have a new style in mind!"

# BRICK OF SOUND

## Chapter 7

# 'VILLAIN' VS. VILLAIN

MADISON WAS WALKING BEHIND CHLOE, TRYING to think of what to say. She then got an idea.

"Yo, Section Leader!" She semi-shouted to her. Chloe turned around. They gave each other a high five.

"What is it, bro?" She asked her.

"I learned how to use above 100 percent without hurting myself!"

"That's really good! What did you do to learn it?"

"Read this!" Madison said, handing her the Power Notes notebook. She opened it up, and began reading it. Once she was done, she handed it back to Madison.

"Thanks, bro! Very cool!" Chloe told her, then walking off.

"Good luck on your match, bro!" Madison shouted to her, giving her a thumbs up. Madison continued to walk to the special section, and sat next to Mandy.

"Go away, weeb."

"Shut up, h."

"We will now begin our second to last quarter final match!" Ms. Martinez announced.

"Do you think she ever gets tired of announcing?" Mandy asked Madison. She shook her head.

"I mean, it's basically her job, besides teaching band."

"I guess that makes sense."

"On our left, we have the previous leader of the Unicorn Villain Corp., which is also known as UVC, Chloe!" Ms. Martinez somewhat shouted into her microphone.

"On our right, we have our district honor band tuba, Allie!"

"You guys can begin...now!" Chloe sent a bunch of waves of energy towards Allie, which she all deflected.

"You're weak!" She said, using all of the energy she deflected to send it back to Chloe. She blocked it, and then quickly thought of a new attack.

"Rainbow Hammer!" She shouted, using her power to create a large hammer purely out of energy. She used a similar tactic that she used during the mini annual tournament, teleporting above Allie.

"Well, who's the weak one now?" Chloe said, slamming the hammer on top of her. This caused a large explosion, so she backed up a bunch. This was her biggest mistake. Allie appeared in front of Chloe.

"You're the weak one." She said, then using her eyes to stun Chloe with some sort of attack.

"Jokes on you…" Chloe began, starting to break the invisible chains with her arms.

"Stun attacks don't work on me!" She finished, finally breaking them and using a large blast to send herself upwards.

"Now that she's in the air, any of Allie's basic moves doesn't work." Madison mumbled, writing things in her Orange Juice Recipes book.

"The only thing that works now," Madison stopped writing for a second. "is that move." Allie charged up some sort of energy that clearly wasn't hers.

"Die!" She shouted upwards, sending a larger wave of energy up to Chloe. Chloe lifted her arms to try and block it. The blast then collided with her. Once the smoke cleared from the blast, she began falling down to the ground, clearly almost defeated.

*Flashback*

Madison was in her bed, basically covered in bandages from her past fight. Chloe was sitting down in a chair that was right next to her.

"Hey, I have a deal for you." She said to her, catching her attention.

"What is it, bro?" Chloe asked her. Madison began smiling with no complete context as to why.

"Until you become the Bari, I want you to promise me one thing."

"And what's that?" Madison lifted her hand up to her.

"Don't ever lose to anyone from district honor band. That's what it is!" She said to her. Chloe shook her hand.

"Okay, I'll do it!"

Chloe slowly began getting up. Before she could use any moves that would change the outcome of if she won or not, she began falling down again.

"I'm sorry…" She mumbled, before dropping back on the floor. She looked up at Madison, who was surprised about how she lost. But, it was the inevitable. You just can't win against the Big Three.

"I couldn't go through with my promise." She passed out.

"She can't lose! She's supposed to be the strongest villain!" Madison thought to herself.

"The winner is Allie!"

## Chapter 8

## HALF EMPTY AND HALF FULL

MADISON SAT IN HER SEAT, BEGINNING TO WRITE down her ideas of outcomes for this fight. She was anticipating this fight, since it's a rivalry that won't be solved in her eyes. She sees them as equals, even if one of them were to win.

"Now for our last match in the quarter finals, we have the two rivals, Brandon and Mandy!" Ms. Martinez announced.

"You ready to settle this?" Brandon said, cracking his knuckles. Mandy sharpened her stop sign with her flames.

"Yeah, just don't chicken out!"

"Alright, you guys can begin… now!" Ms. Martinez finished.

"Bring it on!" Mandy said, charging him. He did the exact same. Once they got close to each other, they both reeled their fists back and punched each other in the face. They stumbled backwards.

She threw her stop sign at him, which left a small cut on his right cheek. Brandon caught the stop sign and threw it back. It left a small cut on her left cheek, and kept on going until it stopped at the arena walls, which it got stuck in.

"Aw, darn it! That's what I was gonna beat you with!" Mandy shouted towards him.

"Suck it up! You'll get another one later!" Brandon retaliated with. "Let's take it up a notch!" Brandon shouted, charging up an impact attack. Mandy would follow suit by charging up a flame. They both would launch their attacks at each other, which clashed. This lasted for a few minutes, until it canceled out.

Mandy grabbed Brandon's arm after charging towards him. She decided to throw him towards the outer ring. He stopped himself using the strength he had.

"Rapid Firing Heat!" She said, shooting multiple mini sized blasts towards him. He deflected them all using pure strength and used that same strength to shoot towards Mandy, without using rockets. He would use a rocket to blast over Mandy when he got close and would charge another impact attack.

"Begone, thot!" He yelled, using a large gust of wind to push her back towards the outer ring. Usually, this attack would be able to even erase people, but this time it just pushed her back.

"Haha, your strongest attack didn't even work on me!" She said, taunting him. She would get into the charging position that activated her power up.

"100% Blaze!" Mandy said, being engulfed in flames. The force of the flames caused Brandon to block the wind from potentially pushing him out. But, this caused him to activate his own power up.

"Full Impact!" Brandon said, using shockwaves similar to Madison's superiority to boost him to full strength. They both stared down each other until they both vanished into the air, having clashes upon clashes.

Madison would be watching this from the audience. She brought her hand up to her face.

"Are they stronger than me?" She asked herself. Mandy used a flame blast to knock him down to the ground. She then would put both of her hands together and begin spinning.

"Tenor Turbo!" Mandy shouted, speeding towards Brandon. He began to get up. His Full Impact would wear off. She separated her hands, which had two mini blasts in them. Once she was right in front of him, she would put them both together into a clapping motion, causing a large explosion.

The smoke had cleared, showing both knocked out on the ground. But soon after, Mandy had gotten up.

"And the winner of this match is Mandy 1.0!" Ms. Martinez announced, earning a great cheer from the crowd. Mandy walked over to Brandon and offered him a hand.

"Right now, we both are the best!" She said to him. He would grab her hand, and she would lift him up.

"When this is over, I want a rematch."

"Yeah okay, but only one." Suddenly, a ship crashed down on the ground. A large ship, around the size of the arena. It landed right next to where they were.

"What the heck, a ship?" Madison asked, standing up. A figure emerged from the top of the ship.

"I declare this tournament over!" The voice announced to everyone, releasing some type of energy that knocked out everyone in the stands except for a few people. Brandon and Mandy looked at them with the same odd glow coming out of their eyes.

"Who the heck do you think you are?" They said at the same time. The figure came more out to where they could be seen.

"I'm 'The Destroyer'," They began. "And I'm here to

take the strongest warrior, who's known as your hero!"

## Chapter 9

# MY HERO

**B**RANDON LOOKED AT MANDY, WHO NODDED IN response. They both got into their fighting stances.

"You're not taking anyone without a fight!" They both said, charging her using full strength.

"I would think twice before trying to fight me." EP Allie told them, holding up her hand. Once they both threw a punch, they were both pushed back with some air force, sending them out of the arena.

"Hey, what're you doing!" Madison yelled down from the audience, jumping off of the railing and landing down on the ground.

"Showing you Earthland weaklings what it means to have power." She responded with. Madison put her hands together, firing off multiple blasts.

"That sure is something you'd say to someone with Power!" She said, teleporting in front of her.

"2.0, don't do it! It's a trap!" Ms. Martinez shouted to her.

"Power Burst!" She said, using the burst aspect to use

a similar gust of wind to attack her. This attack didn't work, however. EP Allie grabbed Madison by the arm that was bandaged and threw her towards the arena. Madison used her hand to stop herself from going any farther. Ms. Martinez stepped in front of Madison.

"What do you want from us? Do you want me?" She asked her. EP Allie agreed by nodding.

"You're the greatest "hero", apparently. None of you guys even know what an actual hero is!" She responded in a somewhat loud voice.

"Then, I'll go with you. I can't make any promises that you will find what you're looking for." Ms. Martinez said, teleporting next to her.

"Wait, no! Don't do this!" Madison finally said, reaching towards the ship. The ship began flying upwards.

"Sorry! I have to do this!" She shouted from above. EP Allie began to charge up an attack that had a dark color similar to 345. She shot it towards Madison, who began to stand up, clearly not ready to block the attack. An explosion went off, as the blast connected.

As the smoke cleared, it showed Mandy blocking the attack. She turned back towards Madison.

"What's wrong? You scared?" Mandy questioned her, in a taunting voice. Madison got up completely.

"Do you even know the situation we're in? If I tried to block that attack, my bones would shatter!" Madison responded with, grabbing Mandy by the collar of the band festival outfit.

"My hero is in danger! Epitomus is in danger! We are all in danger if she's gone! You know that, right!" She finished saying.

"So you have no faith in us? Are you calling all of us weak?" Mandy said, then removing the grip that Madison had.

"Both of you, stop fighting!" Chloe yelled out from the audience seats, flying down to the arena.

"First, we have to plan out everything that we're doing. I still have an old ship from Epitomus that you guys can use. Me on the other hand, I'll be going on my own." She finished, and began walking off.

"I have my own way of getting there. Meet me at the base, Mandy. You're in charge of directions."

"Okay! I heard you!" Mandy said.

"And Madison, I need you to follow Mandy until we get there."

"Fine, I'll go along with the plan." Madison said.

"Glad we could agree on that." She finished, them walking their separate ways.

While at the spaceship, they were waiting on a few people to show up. Mandy was sitting down on the ground, while Madison was on the lookout.

"You're just gonna keep that scar there?" Allie questioned, looking at Mandy's face. The scar from the stop sign had settled, and is now permanent.

"As long as I'm not bleeding to death, I don't care." She answered with her arms crossed.

"I can see why you l- "Allie began, before interrupted by Madison.

"Shut up, stupid."

Some hours later, they all went through with the plan that Chloe had made. They were finally at Epitomus. Madison stepped out of the old ship, and began stretching.

"Woah! This is epic!" She said, looking around. Like Mandy had mentioned, it had a lot more trees than they had. It had more islands, and literally everywhere you turned, you could see water. Mandy emerged from the corridor of the ship to where Madison was.

"You need to calm down with that excitement. We

have an important meeting we need to go to!" She said to Madison, throwing a cup full of ice at her.

"Yeah, so? I just wanted some fresh air!" Madison responded, throwing the cup back at her. Suddenly, out of nowhere, a group of five people arrived on the same island as them.

"I told you guys that the earth landers would be here!" One voice shouted from under the smoke.

"That's only because this is where the coordinates we were given lead to!" Another voice said.

"Come on guys, we have to get into shape! We have two high level earth landers right in front of us!" Madison and Mandy looked at each other.

"Did we encounter aliens or idiots?" Madison asked her.

"I think they're a mix of both." Mandy said in response. Then, the smoke cleared. It was apparently the Kelli Squad, but the Epitomus versions. They were all doing all different poses.

"I'll definitely back you up on that." Madison finished. They both looked at the squad in some form of confusion.

"You dumb earth landers chose the wrong people to fight!" EP Kelli said to them. Madison thought of an idea. She put her right hand over her left.

"Horizontal Slash!" She shouted, sending off a slice like blast that came from in between her hands towards the group.

"Is that....345?" Mandy thought, then backing up. Madison put her right hand into a fist.

"All of our other friends are asleep right now, so we'll take you on!" She shouted to them, having the same odd glow that Mandy and Brandon had during the Band Festival. They looked at her in complete fear.

"Oh! You must've been the wrong person! Let's go guys!" EP Kelli told the rest of her group. Most of them agreed, so they all flew off. The only one that was left was EP Walter.

"Here's a token for having the superiority glow." He said, handing Madison an object, and then immediately flying away. Madison tried putting it on, and it ended up working.

"Epic! I get a scouter!" She somewhat shouted, turning it on. She turned to Mandy.

"How come whenever we find someone, they always give you stuff!" Mandy asked her.

"Maybe it's because you suck." Madison retaliated, laughing after saying that because she thought it was funny.

───────────────

"So, what did you guys do while you arrived?" Chloe asked the two, who both looked at each other. Madison turned to Chloe.

"We fought the Epitomus Kelli Squad that does a bunch of poses!" She said proudly, putting her fist in the air.

"Those guys have been here literally forever! That's so epic!" Chloe responded, giving Madison a high five.

"What do we do if they come back though?" Mandy asked Madison, who gave a thumbs up.

"We show them what it means to be epic, of course!"

# BRICK OF SOUND

## Chapter 10

# THE BIG PLAN

**M**ADISON SAT IN HER SEAT, WAITING FOR EVERY-ONE else to finish coming in. She was ready for this meeting, as Chloe told her she was going to meet someone important. Once they finished sitting down, Chloe stood up.

"Alright, we called you guys to this base because we are beginning a war on those villain rejects!" She announced to everyone.

"Uh, I don't want to lose my superiority this time." A voice similar to Madison's said, causing Madison to look in their direction. It was the person she always wanted to meet. Epitomus Madison.

"It's alright, other Madison. We have a plan." She responded with, reassuring her.

"Yeah, and is it gonna work? Don't you remember what happened last time, to our hero?" A voice similar to Mandy's said. Mandy seemed to already met her, so she didn't care at the moment.

"Of course it's going to work. Don't you have a

brain?" Chloe said to her, which EP Mandy took as a taunt.

"Alright, moving on. So, our plan is going to be like this." She began. She brought out a map of the different islands that were somewhat close to them.

"Madison and her squad will go to the villain base where the Kelli Squad had destroyed. There's still people there." She continued.

"Mandy and Brandon with their squads will go to the separate villain bases that have the most people." She continued, pointing at the two bases.

"And then my squad will directly infiltrate the base where Ms. Martinez is being held." She finished. Madison looked at her.

"Okay, this seems plausible. Maybe if I could train a little more, I'll be prepared." She mumbled, and then continued mumbling about things until Allie threw 'Orange Juice Recipes' at her.

"Anyway, who's squad am I on?" She asked her. Chloe looked at a list that was on the back of the map.

"You, other Madison, other Mandy, and Madison are on the same team. I literally have no trust in you about this, so don't blow up anything." Chloe responded, throwing a device at EP Madison.

"Is this that contact thingy?" She asked, catching it.

"Yeah, so don't try to lose it. I had someone build it for me personally and I don't want it to go to waste."

"Okay."

"The rest of the information is on the back of the map, so you guys can read that after it's over. We have 1 day to prepare for this, alright?" Chloe announced, then getting up to leave.

"We got you, bro!" Madison responded. She then literally walked out of the door. Mandy looked at her and got up to follow her.

"Hey! Get back here!" She shouted, then following her. Once they were outside, Madison stopped walking and turned to Mandy.

"Didn't you learn a new fighting style? Are you gonna use that in the fight?" She asked her.

"It's called Dragon. It's a mix of my Burst attack and Blasts. And of course I am!" Madison answered.

"Alright, then show me it." She stated, causing Madison to back off a little bit.

"No way! If I did use it, I could seriously hurt you!"

"Then fight me instead!" Mandy shouted, grabbing Madison's arm, which caught her by surprise, and soaring off into the sky to another island.

When Mandy got close, she threw Madison down on to the island. Madison used her hand to stop her from continuing to fly. She looked up to Mandy in complete anger and confusion.

"Do you think I want to fight you right now?" She shouted up to her, grabbing her right arm just in case.

"Why do you think I told you that…" Mandy began, suddenly dropping down to the ground, then using a blast to fly towards Madison. She grabbed Madison by the face and set off a blast.

"In the first place!" She finished. Madison released the grip off of her face and charged power in her right arm.

"Powerful Fist!" She shouted, punching her straight in the gut, sending her flying into a large rock. Mandy lifted the rock off of her.

"That's not your full strength!" She yelled towards her, launching off multiple blasts in between her hands in anger. 345 began to activate in Madison's body, starting the line patterns to appear, this time all the way up to her face.

"You really are dumb! You don't understand how my new fighting styles work!" Madison shouted out to Mandy, running towards her.

"Oh yeah? Then show me!" Mandy retaliated, then preparing for the attack. A sudden boost of speed from mysterious steam coming off of Madison's body, that didn't last long, launched her towards Mandy. Now in front of Mandy, she dropped her hands on the ground and tried kicking her upwards.

"A sudden boost in speed?" She thought, barely dodging her kick. Flipping herself back upwards, she reeled back a fist, which was charging energy extremely fast by the second.

"Dragon's Power: Fist of Anger!" She exclaimed, then launching the powerful attack at her. This caused a large amount of energy to radiate off of the explosion. As the smoke from the attack cleared, it showed Madison with her arm pointing down to Mandy, who was now on the ground.

"Once I learn a new fighting style, I can't take the damage myself." She said, showing her how somehow both of her arms were basically broken, and that she was trembling.

"I'll get payback-" She began, then collapsing onto the ground from the pain. Mandy got up and picked up Madison.

"Maybe, but not now."

---

Mandy arrived at the base and dropped Madison on the floor. Chloe ran up to her.

"What did you do? Don't tell me you fought her again!" Chloe asked, looking at her.

"Even though her body resigned, she still looks peaceful while asleep." Mandy answered, pointing at her. Chloe noticed how she was basically sleeping like a baby, even though she always claims being very strong.

"Why did you even push her to that point in the first place?" She asked. Mandy walked over to where her room was, and opened the door.

"So, she could see how she needs to get stronger if she wants to protect everyone."

# BRICK OF SOUND

## Chapter 11

# INTRODUCING THE KELLI SQUAD

MEANWHILE, WHILE EVERYONE ELSE WAS AT Epitomus, there still were people left by them at Earthland to keep the school and everything else safe. The most predominant, however, were the Kelli squad. They were put together by Madison herself.

*Flashback*

"Wait, what are we supposed to do while you guys are gone?" Kelli asked Madison, who opened up her 'Orange Juice Recipes' to a specific page. She showed it to them, and it had an odd concept drawing of a 5-person squad doing what she would call 'epic poses,'

"You guys will keep the school safe!" She said, giving a big thumbs up. She handed the notebook to Walter

61

and stood up.

"If you want to be very epic, then everything you do has to have that little 'Impact!' to it!" Madison shouted, then imitating how Brandon used his one named attack.

"That's a good idea!" Kandi agreed, then doing the t-pose, which caused Madison to laugh.

"Then, what's this 'squad' called?" Walter asked, looking at the pages that she wrote, then handing it back.

"The 'Kelli Squad,' of course!" She shouted, this time even louder, putting her fist in the air.

"And the secret is..." She began, bringing her fist down. "...is that you all have something in common!"

"Alright, one more time guys! Introducing the Kelli Squad!" Kelli began, doing a pose, that again, Madison would call epic.

"Walter!" He shouted, doing a pose also.

"Enza!"

"Aaliyah." She said, literally not in the spirit of the poses, but still doing it anyway.

"Kandi!"

"...and Kelli! We are the...." Kelli continued. They all suddenly got into different poses.

"Kelli Squad!" They almost all shouted, and had a perfectly timed firework go off behind them, even though it was literally broad daylight.

"I told you guys we shined bright! Even Ms. Martinez would be proud!" Kelli proudly said, pointing up to the air.

"That's if she doesn't decide to resign." Aaliyah said.

"Don't say that! We all know that she won't ever lose!" Enza responded.

"Guys, you do realize that we're gonna need a plan if

we want to continue this squad thing until they come back, right?" Walter asked them. Kelli then turned around.

"All we can do right now is hope that this page that Madison handed to us will actually work." She answered, putting it down on the ground. The page had many notes on it that happened to all be written by Madison, but one note that stood out.

"How are we supposed to know how to beat an enemy that defeated many heroes stronger than us?" Kandi asked. Kelli threw the paper in the air.

"She said to use the art of surprise!" She called out.

## Meanwhile in Epitomus

Madison woke up, and seemed to had forgotten what had happened the day before. She got up out of her bed and headed to the living room. Chloe looked at her.

"Good timing, bro! We were just about to begin eating!" She said to Madison. Madison looked around in confusion, since she was still trying to focus while half asleep.

"What time is it?" She asked, walking over to a chair and sitting in it.

"It's around 6 PM, why?" Chloe said, causing Madison to fall out of her chair. She then got back up, and seemed to had woken up completely.

"Why didn't you wake me up if you had food?" She yelled, lifting the chair back up and then sitting down in it again. Mandy put her empty cup away from her mouth.

"Cause you probably would've found something to complain about." She answered. Chloe handed Madison a plate, which had a decent amount of food on it. Before she began eating it, Mandy took the plate and ate everything off of it, then put it down.

"Hey! What the heck?" Madison asked, grabbing Mandy by the jacket that she had received that was specifically made for Epitomus.

"I told you that you were gonna complain about something!" She retaliated, then getting into a mini fight with her.

## Back on Earthland

"While Madison and the others are gone, we are gonna show the world that even the weaker ones are strong!" Kelli shouted upwards, then putting on her new goggles that Ms. Martinez had gave her.

"Then, Ms. Martinez will come back and notice how strong we really are!"

## Chapter 12

## THE THREE 6TH GRADERS

ADISON HAD FINALLY PUT ON HER EPITOMUS outfit that she doesn't want to wear for a long time, since Mandy gave it to her. She walked outside of the ship to meet with the members of her squad.

"So, other Madison, can you fly?" She asked EP Madison, who began to float. She gave her a thumbs up.

"Of course I can! Everyone in Epitomus can fly!" She proudly answered, and Madison grinned with full excitement and amazement, which she doesn't usually have.

"That's epic!" She shouted.

"You wanna know what else is epic?" EP Madison asked her, taking off the damaged cape that she had on.

"You wearing this!" She exclaimed, putting the cape on her. EP Mandy picked up a small rock and threw it at her head.

"Don't you know that we have to go soon?" She told EP Madison, who just smiled in response.

"Come on, just let us enjoy the fun that we're having!

It probably won't last that long, you know!" EP Madison responded. While all of this was going on, Allie was sitting on a rock while reading through 'Orange Juice Recipes'.

"Fine, I'll give you guys a few minutes. But we're leaving right after that!" EP Mandy said.

They finally arrived at the destroyed base, but Chloe was wrong. There were literally no people to be found. Madison picked up some of the rubble, which easily fell out of her hand.

"This damage is new. Judging on the surroundings, we aren't the only people here." She said, then throwing the rubble at a specific spot.

"Good eyesight, young hero!" EP Allie said, then appearing completely out of nowhere.

"I don't take compliments from people like you." She said, charging a very small blast in her hand.

"You're supposed to be at your base! Why are you here?" EP Madison angrily asked, activating her superiority.

"I just wanted to see how the future number one hero is." She answered, then looking at Madison. She activated some sort of attack that caused Madison to stop charging the attack and grabbing her eyes.

"Other Madison! Isn't Power supposed to be immune to those attacks?" Allie asked her. She nodded in response.

"Yeah, but she's targeting something that isn't Power!" Madison stopped what she was doing, and grabbed her right arm instead.

"You have no control over me!" She shouted, using a burst attack to its extent, which put a lot of pain in her arm.

"No one has escaped my mind control before." EP Allie thought. Since she was focusing on Madison, EP Madison took this chance to teleport in front of her.

"Shockwaves: Kick Force!" She exclaimed, using the force of the shockwaves to force her backwards. This made

Madison finally gain full control over her body, but before she could so anything, EP Mandy continued the attack that EP Madison did,

"Full Power Heat Wave!" She shouted, using her left hand to launch a large wave of energy towards EP Allie.

While this was happening, Mandy and Brandon were both walking throughout Epitomus, trying to figure out where they were.

"Uh, I think we're lost." They both said at the same time, then looking at each other.

"Hey! Why are you here?" Brandon asked, pointing at Mandy.

"No, why are you here?" Mandy asked, pointing back at Brandon.

"How about we settle this right now?" Brandon shouted, rolling up his sleeve of his new jacket for Epitomus.

"Heck yeah!" A large crash was heard, causing them to both look towards the source. It was a smaller ship.

"Brandon! Why are you here?" A voice asked, emerging from the ship. They were recognized as Karla, the strongest of the 6th graders.

"Oh yeah, you're Madison's friend." Mandy said, lowering her arm, then crossing her arms.

"Didn't she tell you? She's also my sister." Brandon told her. She looked at him and began laughing.

"Now you have something to take care of while in another dimension!" She said, continuing to laugh.

"Karla, stop leaving us behind in the ship!" Another voice said, coming from inside of the ship. The two people were identified as Kandace and Charlie, the other two members of the 3-person squad.

"How did you guys get here in the first place?" Mandy questioned, since she was very confused.

"Well, first we saw this really weird group of people."

*Flashback*

"Exploding Toilet!" Kelli called out, sending a barrage of water bullets into the air. She then looked at a sheet of paper that was written by Madison.

"She said that oddly named moves have to be more powerful than regular ones! Why is this my weaker move?" She shouted.

"Well, why don't you test it out on something?" Kandi asked her. Kelli put on the goggles and began looking around. She was able to see something that was moving so fast to the point that the regular eye couldn't find it.

"Exploding Toilet!" She called out again, sending a barrage of water bullets towards it, in hopes of getting a single hit in. However, all of them ended up hitting them.

"Ow! Why'd you hit me?" Charlie asked, as he was the one moving that fast. Everyone else looked at him confused.

"Who even are you, kid?" Walter asked him. He got up from off the ground, and looked at all of them until he got an idea on what to say.

"I'm Madison's friend!" He said, showing them a piece of paper that had Madison's signature on it. They all looked at it.

"It does look like her handwriting." Enza said, and they all nodded in agreement. Karla and Kandace showed up.

"They're from the annual tournament!" Kelli said. Karla picked up Charlie barely any effort.

"Do you guys know where Madison is?" She asked them.

"Yeah, she's in another dimension." Aaliyah answered her.

"Alright, let's go guys!" Karla exclaimed, and they all blasted off using their powers.

"Those two are just like Madison and Chloe." Kandi said, and they all agreed.

"We could tell by just meeting them."

"...and then we found a spaceship, so we tried to use it, and that's how we ended up here!" Karla finished.

"You should head towards their main base, they're gonna need some extra support there." Mandy responded to them. They all headed to the ship that they came in.

"Hey, shouldn't we be doing the thing that we were supposed to?" Brandon asked her.

"Oh. I forgot."

# BRICK OF SOUND

## Chapter 13

# THE BROKEN PLAN

ADISON LOOKED TO HER RIGHT. SHE SAW SOME oddly placed crystals, and got an idea that probably wouldn't work, like usual. She teleported over to them, and picked up one.

"Time to eat a foreign object!" She said, putting it up to her mouth and biting it. Once she did this, the aura of Power surrounded her at a more rapid pace than normal.

"Those are Power crystals! You aren't supposed to eat those!" EP Madison called out to her, but Madison just ignored. She then dropped the crystal on the ground, and the bandages that were on her arms had come off, showing the linear pattern of 345.

"I think Power had a reaction with something else." EP Mandy said. Allie remembered a page that she read from 'Orange Juice Recipes'.

"It's 345." She thought. Madison got into a similar powering up position to when Mandy used 100% Blaze, and charged up a lot of energy, until the rapid aura changed into a gusty wind force, mixed with the aura of the curse.

She shot a sharp wave of wind towards EP Allie, which she raised her arms to block. The attack still went through, as it was stronger than the wind attacks that she used.

"I knew that you were the hero I was looking for. Show me more!" EP Allie shouted towards her. Madison let out a shout, and charged towards her. She landed a punch on her, and then another, then another, until eventually she pushed her back.

"Madison isn't this strong. Last time I checked, she couldn't even get close to any of the low reeds without being blasted, all 4 of them." Allie stated, as Madison launched herself towards EP Allie.

"Right now, she could probably beat me at 50% of my power." EP Madison continued for her. Madison charged up something similar to her horizontal slash, but it was larger. Without usually naming the attack, she just shot it towards her. EP Allie did dodge, but when she moved out the way, Madison teleported behind her and used a swift kick to hit her across the face.

## *In Power World*

"Who the heck are you?" Madison asked someone who also looked like her. They were sitting down in chairs, and for some reason, drinking tea.

"You, but not you. I'm that curse that you have no control over having." '345' Madison answered.

"So, now there's 3 of me? Are there more?" She questioned.

"Surprisingly, no. But you never know, there probably is another one somewhere."

"I have a lot of questions for you, but I'd rather ask those later if I get a chance. One more question though…."

"What is it?"

"Aren't you supposed to like, fight me or something?"

## Back in Epitomus

Madison finally gained control over her body, so the line pattern had slowly vanished away.

"Uh, is this still Epitomus?" She asked, looking around until she saw EP Allie on the ground. The communication device that EP Madison got went off, so she turned it on.

"Hey guys, we need some back up here." Chloe said from the device, which had a low-quality sound, making Madison laugh, despite the somewhat serious situation.

"Okay, we're on it." EP Madison answered, turning it back off. EP Allie had begun vanishing.

"You guys were fooled!" She shouted, laughing maniacally, then disappearing. Madison turned to Allie.

"You see, this is why we didn't believe you when you said that you weren't 'The Destroyer'." She said.

"That makes no sense." Allie responded.

"Says the actual child." EP Madison grabbed Madison by the arm and began floating.

"We got to go to the main base, I think they're in trouble." She said, soaring off in to the sky.

"You have to teach me how to fly sometime!" Madison told her, causing EP Madison to grin.

"I'll teach you when this plan is over!"

Once they all arrived at the base, it looked relatively new. The only thing that Madison found interesting was a rock that she found, that was later threw in the water by Allie. Chloe showed up, and so did everyone else that was a part of the plan.

"So, why are we all here?" Mandy asked Chloe. She pointed towards the middle of the base. EP Allie appeared out of thin air, with Ms. Martinez with the power chains on.

"We have to get her away from her successfully." She

answered, beginning to think of a good idea.

"How about we just charge right in?" Madison said, firing off blasts from her hands.

"No!" Everyone but EP Madison shouted at her.

"I mean, it's a good idea if you think about it. We can use the art of surprise to show her how strong we really are!" EP Madison said, high fiving Madison.

"I know! How about we trust someone with a little of our energy to use a final attack that'll end it?" Chloe asked everyone, causing Madison to cross her arms.

"That's very cliche. It sounds very familiar, but I don't know where it came from." She answered, then walking into the base.

"I'll go by myself."

## Meanwhile in Earthland

"I'm the new leader of the strongest villain association!" A figure called out. Walter looked at them.

"You're like, 2 feet tall." He said.

"That's an over exaggeration!"

"Does anyone even know his name?" Kelli asked the rest of the squad.

"Of course you do! I'm the new strongest villain, Kendall!"

## Chapter 14

## CURSE SEAL

MADISON GOT CLOSER TO THE TWO, UNTIL SHE decided to stop walking. She lifted up her right hand, and started to fire off many mini blasts.

"So, what'll it take for me to get my hero back?" Madison asked her, clenching her fist.

"Your hero? She's not a true hero." EP Allie said, beginning to activate some sort of power.

"Yeah she is! She saved all of us!" She shouted at her.

"You know what? I'll just straight up tell you this. You are the true hero." She responded, beginning to release the power chains.

"You have Power! That's what makes you the better hero." She continued. Madison dropped her fist to her side.

"No way am I a true hero! I haven't saved anyone, not once!" Madison charged towards her. EP Allie set off a large explosion which completely decimated the base, causing Madison to lift her arms to block.

## Meanwhile in Earthland

"Phoenix Flame!" Kendall shouted, sending off a large outwards wave of energy similar to Mandy's blazes.

"A Mythical type, just like me." Kelli said, pointing her arms towards him, then looking back at the rest of her squad.

"You guys can just sit back and watch!" She continued, sending off a large wave of water, then looking back at him.

"Cause this is going to be a great time!" She finished.

## Back in Epitomus

"So how's it been, 2.0?" Ms. Martinez asked, grabbing her shoulder and activating the Sun power. Madison grinned in excitement.

"Ms. Martinez! You're back!" She exclaimed, taking the jacket off and putting the cape back on. Ms. Martinez sent off a large wave of heat, similar to EP Mandy's attacks, but much stronger.

"I told you guys it would work." EP Madison said to everyone. Madison ran towards EP Allie for a second time.

"You're making a big mistake." EP Allie said, charging energy that was the same as 345's. Madison ignored this however, and began reeling back a fist, using Power to make it stronger.

"That's another trap!" Ms. Martinez shouted towards her, but Madison still went on. EP Allie punched Madison in the stomach, which sent a large shock of power into her body. This sent her flying backwards, back to where Ms. Martinez was.

## In Power World

Another seat appeared next to the table, confusing 345 Madison. Madison appeared in her chair, then EP Allie appeared in the new seat.

"Why are you here?" 345 Madison asked, putting down her cup of tea. EP Allie looked at her.

"I'm here to tell you guys the future." She answered. Madison looked at her in confusion.

"Alright. I'll listen." Madison said, and the other agreed.

## *In Epitomus*

"2.0! Wake up!" Ms. Martinez said, shaking Madison. This didn't work however, and EP Allie walked towards them, charging up the curse energy.

"This'll be your last day as number one hero!" She shouted. Ms. Martinez used the Sun Power to set off a bright flare, which blinded everyone else, but not EP Allie.

"This will be your last day in Epitomus!" She called out, punching the ground, and put all of her energy into it. This caused a large crack to open up, and it began to burn up from all of the heat. EP Allie still went on.

"Alright, let's go guys!" Chloe told everyone, causing most of them to fly off to the ship. Ms. Martinez stood up, which made EP Allie stop walking.

"A true hero dies protecting what's most important to them." She said. Madison began to wake up.

"You're not a true hero!" EP Allie shouted, blasting the energy towards her.      Ms. Martinez looked back to Madison.

"You are the true hero." She said, smiling, even while facing death itself. Madison reached her arm towards her.

"Wait! You have to come back with us!" She said, and then the blast collided. Madison waited for the smoke to clear to see the outcome. As the smoke cleared, she still saw

Ms. Martinez standing proud, like how she usually did. EP Allie looked at Madison.

"True hero, that's now a person that you couldn't save! After all of this hard work, you still couldn't complete a simple task!" She shouted towards her. Madison processed everything. It was similar to what she told her in Power World, yet it was something completely different, and that it would happen later.

"Madison, I told you that you wouldn't get me back." Mandy said, using the blazes to take up most of her body and grabbing Madison. She then flew off to the ship. Brandon walked through the dark energy completely unharmed.

"I'll show you why I'm stronger than Mandy!" He shouted, putting his fists together.

"True Impact or True Idiot? Which one is it?" EP Allie asked him, turning off the 345 energy.

"I'm True Impact!" Brandon answered, punching the air, sending off a large gust of wind that was more powerful than usual.

"This has to be Super Superiority." EP Allie thought, walking towards him. He lifted up his right hand.

"Begone, thot!" He shouted, using an even stronger gust of wind to send her backwards. This time, the erase effect worked.

"I'll get you back for this. You aren't even a hero!" She said, then disappearing into thin air.

"You're a hero because you just saved everyone!" A voice similar to Ms. Martinez said, grabbing his shoulder. He looked back to them.

"Ms. Martinez? I thought you died!" Brandon asked her. Ms. Martinez brought her hand up to her forehead.

"That was my Epitomus counterpart!" She proudly said, then teleporting both of them back to Earthland.

Everyone was gathered into the spaceship, and began

leaving back to Earthland. Madison looked out the window.

"Other Madison! Why aren't you coming back?" She shouted out, hoping that it would reach her.

"I feel like it's my time to go now. Along with everyone of Epitomus, and Epitomus itself." She said, to where it could only be heard by Madison.

"But, you were supposed to teach me how to fly!" She called out. Epitomus began exploding.

"All you have to do, other Madison, is to believe!" She said, then it exploded, right when the ship made it to Earthland.

Madison ran out of the ship while it was still in the air, and landed on the ground. She looked towards the villain that the Kelli Squad was fighting.

"Madison, you're back already?" Kelli asked her. Madison pointed towards the villain.

"I'll show you the reason why you're a bad villain!" She shouted to him.

### The Band House

Meanwhile, the ship had landed next to the band house. Chloe walked out, looking to find EP Chloe.

"She must've already disappeared." She said, sitting down on the ground, looking in utter defeat. Mandy walked up to her and patted her on the back.

"Don't worry, it wasn't your fault."

### Back with the Kelli Squad

Madison had grabbed Kendall by his face and blasted him until he hit the floor. She got up after doing this.

"You should join us!" She proudly said to him, reaching her hand towards him. He got up and wiped away the smoke from his face.

"That sounds like a good idea!" He responded, shaking Madison's hand. The Kelli Squad looked at them in surprise.

"How does she even do that?" Walter asked the rest of them. Madison walked up to Kelli and gave her a high five.

"You guys are the best squad I've ever seen! I hope you guys do good in the future!"

## Chapter 15

## DAY AFTER DISASTER

**M**ADISON SAT IN A CHAIR AND BEGAN WRITING things in 'Orange Juice Recipes'. She has very late reactions, so nothing really phases her. It was almost like nothing had happened.

She decided to check her phone to see if anything had happened, and then it hit her.

"Oh yeah, today's my birthday." She said, in her regular unenthusiastic voice. Madison put her phone back down and continued writing in the notebook.

"Oh, wait! Today's my birthday!" She called out. She then heard a knock on the door, and then opened it.

"Guess who's back?" Ms. Martinez said to her, walking inside. Madison looked at her with excitement.

"You're so epic!" Madison exclaimed.

"So, where is everyone?" She asked.

"They left me here to take care of the band house while they investigated something that had happened."

"And what was that?"

"They think EP Allie is back." She answered. She

handed Ms. Martinez a cup of tea.

"Nice."

"I know."

## In a forest near the school

"Chloe, try searching for them using that ability you learned in Epitomus." Mandy told her.

"I'm telling you, I can't sense any energy." Chloe answered her. Kelli put her goggles on to try and find anyone invisible.

"I found someone!" She said, pointing towards a tree. They looked towards the tree until the person finally revealed themselves.

"It feels great to be free!" They shouted out. It was revealed to be 345 Madison. Chloe charged up some of her energy.

"Tell us where that disgrace to villains is!" She said, charging towards her. As she threw the punch, 345 Madison jumped over her.

"Sorry, but I was told to not give away any information." She answered. Mandy appeared above her and tried to blast her from above, but she still dodged it. She then grabbed Mandy and threw her into Chloe.

"You're not Madison! Who are you?" Mandy asked her. She activated the line part to 345, with a new addition of the glow similar to what Madison had.

"I'm 345 itself!"

## Back at the Band House

"Hey, Ms. Martinez! Teach me how to sense energy!" Madison said, firing off mini blasts from her hands.

"Okay, I'll teach you." She agreed in response. Suddenly, an explosion was heard from afar.

"Never mind!" She shouted, grabbing Madison's arm

and teleporting to where she heard it. She dropped Madison and looked around for the person who caused it. Ms. Martinez then looked to her right, to see 345 Madison with her hand right next to her face.

"Madison's hero!" She called out, then firing off a blast full of the dark energy of 345. Madison ran over to where Chloe was.

"I don't know how she escaped Power World!" Madison told her, unable to explain the situation.

"Well, the real question is, how is Ms. Martinez back?" She asked her. Madison just continued to watch. Ms. Martinez activated the Erase effect that she doesn't use regularly, which canceled out 345. She then grabbed 345 Madison's arm and face and pinned her down to the ground.

"What business do you have with us?" She questioned her. 345 Madison looked up to her.

"Just doing what I was assigned to do." She answered. Finally, EP Allie had appeared in the air.

"Looks like you survived, fake hero!" She shouted down to Ms. Martinez, who didn't care.

"Looks like you survived, dumb villain." She responded. EP Allie snapped her fingers, and 345 Madison appeared right next to her.

"We'll be leaving now. But, we're going to have to take something." She said, generating a very small blast in her hand. Madison had been teleported by her, and was now being teleported with them.

"Give her back!" Mandy called up to them. 345 Madison used the dark energy to surround them.

"I'll tell you guys one thing." Madison began.

"Don't come back for me."